Firefighters

Sandy Sepehri

FITZGERALD BOOKS

Bethany, Missouri

Photo Credits:
Cover © Graham Prentice; Title Page © Lane Erickson; Page 4 © Shaun Lowe; Page 5 © Dale A Stork,
Neo Edmund; Page 6 © Jason Lugo; Page 7 © Bryan Eastham, Jason Lugo; Page 8 © The Image Area,
Brandon Clark; Page 9 © Stephen Coburn, Shaun Lowe; Page 10 © The Image Area; Page 11 © Condor 36,
Robert Pernell; Pages 12, 13 © GSK; Page 14 © Peter Hansen; Page 15 © Nir Levy, Page 16 © Mitch Aunger,
Sarah Cates; Page 17 © Todd S. Holder; Page 19 © Shaun Lowe; Page 21 © Bob McMillan/ FEMA Photo;
Page 22 © Zimmytws

Cataloging-in-Publication Data

Sepehri, Sandy
    Firefighters / Sandy Sepehri. — 1st ed.
    p. cm. — (Community helpers)

    Includes bibliographical references and index.
    Summary: Text and photographs introduce firefighters,
from their work, clothing, and tools, to how fires are extinguished
and becoming a firefighter.
    ISBN-13: 978-1-4242-1354-2 (lib. bdg. : alk. paper)
    ISBN-10: 1-4242-1354-1 (lib. bdg. : alk. paper)
    ISBN-13: 978-1-4242-1444-0 (pbk. : alk. paper)
    ISBN-10: 1-4242-1444-0 (pbk. : alk. paper)

    1. Fire fighters—Juvenile literature. 2. Fire extinction—Juvenile literature.
3. Fire extinction—Vocational guidance—Juvenile literature. [1. Fire fighters.
2. Fire extinction. 3. Fire extinction—Vocational guidance.
4. Occupations.] I. Sepehri, Sandy. II. Title. III. Series.
    TH9148.S47 2007
    628.9'25—dc22

First edition
© 2007 Fitzgerald Books
802 N. 41st Street, P.O. Box 505
Bethany, MO 64424, U.S.A.
Printed in China
Library of Congress Control Number: 2007900210

Table of Contents

What Do Firefighters Do?

Firefighters protect people and property from fires.

What Do Firefighters Wear?

Firefighters wear clothes that protect them from fire. Their masks protect them from **smoke inhalation**.

Firefighters also wear a helmet and boots to protect them.

Firefighters' Equipment

Firefighters use special equipment to help them with their jobs. An axe is used to cut holes in buildings.

Burning buildings are full of **toxic** smoke. Firefighters must wear masks to help them breathe air with **oxygen**.

9

Firefighters use a hose to spray water on a fire.

The fire hose attaches to a pump truck. The pump truck sucks water from a fire hydrant.

Fire Trucks

Fire trucks are used to pump water. But they are also a firefighter's transportation and tool box.

Fire trucks carry all of the gear that a firefighter needs to put out a fire.

Fire trucks carry hoses, axes, ladders, and first aid kits.

Fire Stations

A fire station is a building where firefighters work. They store their truck and firefighting gear in the fire station.

Fire stations are all shapes and sizes.
What does your local fire station look like?

How Are Fires Extinguished?

There are three ways to **extinguish** a fire:
1. Cool the fire.
2. **Smother** the fire.
3. Separate the fuel from the fire.

The fuel for a fire can be a chemical,
like gasoline, or a solid, like wood.

Becoming a Firefighter

Firefighters have dangerous jobs. They risk their lives to help others. With the proper training, anyone can become a firefighter.

You can train to fight fires in cities or in forests.

Fire Safety at Home

Everyone can practice fire safety. Learn how to call 911. Every house should have a fire extinguisher.

Glossary

extinguish (ex TING wish) — to put out a fire

oxygen (OX eh gin) — an element in the air we breathe

smoke inhalation (SMOKE in hal AY shun) — to breathe in smoke

smother (SMUTH ur) — to cover something thickly

toxic (TOK sik) — poisonous

Index

FURTHER READING

Englart, Mindi. *How Do I Become A Firefighter?* Blackbirch Press, 2002.
Hamilton, Kersten. *Firefighters to the Rescue*. Viking Juvenile, 2005.

WEBSITES TO VISIT

Because Internet links change so often, Fitzgerald Books has developed an online list of websites related to the subject of this book. This site is updated regularly. Please use this link to access the list: www.fitzgeraldbookslinks.com/ch/fir

ABOUT THE AUTHOR

Sandy Sepehri is an honors graduate from the University of Central Florida. She has authored several children's books and is a columnist for a parents' magazine.